Pearlie in Central Park

WENDY HARMER

Illustrated by Gypsy Taylor

RANDOM HOUSE AUSTRALIA

For my two central Park fairies — Misty and Riley.

A Random House book
Published by Random House Australia Pty Ltd
Level 3, 100 Pacific Highway, North Sydney NSW 2060
www.randomhouse.com.au

First published by Random House Australia in 2010

Addresses for companies within the Random House Group can be found
at www.randomhouse.com.au/offices.

National Library of Australia
Cataloguing-in-Publication Entry

Harmer, Wendy
Pearlie in Central Park / Wendy Harmer; illustrator Gypsy Taylor
ISBN 978 1 74166 377 8 (pbk.)
Series: Harmer, Wendy. Pearlie the park fairy; 11
Target audience: For children
Subjects: Fairies – Juvenile fiction
Central Park (New York, N.Y.) – Juvenile fiction
Other authors/contributors: Taylor, Gypsy

A823.4

Designed and typeset by Jobi Murphy
Printed and bound by Everbest Printing Co.Ltd, China

It was a crisp winter morning and Pearlie was riding high in the sky on Queen Emerald's magic ladybird. Her home was far, far away. Down below, she could see the whole of Central Park, New York City.

'Hurly-burly!' cried Pearlie. 'This place is huge! Crystal must be the busiest fairy ever.'

As she flew closer, Pearlie was amazed to see that everything was covered in sparkling snow. She had heard about snow, but it had never fallen in Jubilee Park.

'Frost and icicles!' exclaimed Pearlie. 'How beautiful!'

Queen Emerald herself had arranged for Pearlie to stay with Crystal the Central Park Fairy for a wonderful winter holiday. The ladybird landed on a deep snowdrift and watched as Pearlie took her map and set off to find Cherry Hill.

From across an icy lake Pearlie spotted a magnificent black and gold fountain.

'Oooh! There's Crystal's place!' she cried.

She hurried towards it and was surprised to see that right on the tippy top, sitting on a round glass lamp, was a small furry creature. It had the cutest face ever, handsome whiskers and a large bushy tail.

It was one of the famous grey squirrels of Central Park.

'Hiya! I'm Chester,' he called. 'You must be Pearlie. We've been waiting for you.'

'Hello there,' said Pearlie.

'It's real kind of you to look after the park while Crystal's away on her vacation,' Chester smiled.

'Pardon?' gasped Pearlie. 'I thought I would be staying with Crystal. Isn't she here?'

'Dang!' said Chester. 'There must be some mistake. Crystal's flown off to Hawaii. But she asked me to give you this.'

Chester gave Pearlie a note, and this is what it said:

Queen Emerald's ladybird flew off at once with the news.

An icy wind blew through Central Park. Pearlie pulled her coat tightly about her as big fat snowflakes swirled through the air and fell on her head.

'Brrrr …' Pearlie shivered. 'How will I ever manage? I've never looked after a park this big before.'

'Now, don't you fuss,' said Chester. 'Me and my buddies will help. You better come on in before you turn into a purple popsicle!'

Chester leapt from the fountain, scurried along a bare branch and disappeared through a hole in the trunk of an old oak tree.

Pearlie picked up her suitcase and flew after him. Through the hole and down, down, down she fluttered in the dark until she landed with a 'bump' on the floor of the squirrels' den.

Pearlie dusted off her coat and saw four big eyes staring at her.

'Say "howdy" to my friends Misty and Maple,' said Chester.

'We know all about you, Pearlie,' Maple sweetly cooed. 'Why, you're as pretty as a picture.'

Pearlie blushed madly.

'You're just in time,' said Misty. 'Please share our supper.'

Misty put a small walnut on the table and the three squirrels eyed it hungrily. It didn't seem enough for everyone.

'The snow came early this year,' explained Chester. 'I wish we'd stored more nuts and acorns to last the long winter.'

'We might find a morsel or two buried under the ice and snow,' Maple added. 'And when spring comes, there will be flower buds to nibble.'

'I hope the season changes real soon,' sighed Misty. 'I'm famished!'

Pearlie felt sad for the squirrels. They did look awfully thin and spring seemed a long way off.

'I have some rose petal muffins in my bag,' she said. 'I made them myself. Would you like to share?'

'Yes, please!' cheered the squirrels.

They held the muffins in their delicate paws and munched happily.

When the squirrels' tummies were full, they chattered to Pearlie about this and that and then settled down to sleep in a soft and furry heap.

But Pearlie was wide awake. Even if she was
a stranger in Central Park, she had to help her
new friends! She would see to it first thing in
the morning.

Pearlie was up at dawn. She watched as the squirrels dug busily through the snowdrifts and found nothing to eat at all.

Suddenly, Pearlie heard squawking. She peered through the frosty bushes and saw a crowd of birds noisily pecking at a feeder filled to the top with delicious sunflower seeds.

As she flew closer the birds spied her with glittering eyes.

'Caw, caw! Who are YOU?' the birds screeched. 'Go away!'

'Excuse me,' said Pearlie politely. 'Can you spare any seeds for some starving squirrels?'

'GET LOST!' the nasty birds shouted. 'This food is for US!'

They flapped their wings and swiped at Pearlie with their claws. Pearlie dodged their cruel, sharp beaks and flew to a nearby tree.

How could she get those selfish creatures to share their food? Even if she zapped the birds with her wand, she still wouldn't be able to get the seeds out. The opening was simply too small for a fairy to squeeze through.

And then Pearlie had a very good idea.

She flew down to the snow-covered grass and called to the squirrels.

'Chester, Misty, Maple!'

When they had all gathered, she told them her plan.

'Just like the birds, we'll sing for our supper,' explained Pearlie. 'We'll put on a show. It's what we do back home in Jubilee Park. Let's go!'

The three squirrels clapped their paws and bounded after Pearlie, their bushy tails twitching with excitement.

That afternoon, when the birds of Central Park flew over Cherry Hill, their beady eyes spied a poster on a tree trunk.

THE
AMAZING!
the AWESOME!
Squirrels on ICE!!
COME ONE, COME ALL
DONATION: Sunflower seeds

A blue jay, who was the greediest of all the birds, cackled with laughter.

'Squirrels can't skate!' he shrieked at Pearlie. 'I'm not paying one good seed until I see those fur balls twirl!'

Now Pearlie was more determined than ever to convince the birds to give their sunflower seeds to see the show. All afternoon she watched Chester, Maple and Misty practise their skating moves on the ice-filled fountain. She helped them up whenever they landed with a furry THUD!

Later, when the sun had disappeared behind dark clouds, the lamps on the Cherry Hill fountain glowed brightly.

The jays, the woodpeckers, the wrens and the finches crowded on every branch. They were twittering with curiosity.

Pearlie had used her magic to decorate the golden flowers and bluestone bowls of the fountain with frozen spider webs. Icy dewdrops shone like diamonds in the lamplight.

But Chester was nervous. 'Can we do it, Pearlie?' he asked.

'Yes we can!' Pearlie declared.

Her wand flashed and beautiful music wafted through the freezing night air.

Misty and Maple appeared in shimmering costumes. They sped across the ice paw in paw, waltzing and looping around each other with amazing grace.

The fat blue jay fell off his perch in surprise and bounced on the ice. 'Awwk!'

'Tweet, tweet! Chirp, chirp! Go Misty! Go Maple!' the other birds whooped in wonder.

Then came Chester in a bow tie and top hat.
He leapt and spun like a champion using his
bushy tail to steady himself. Double … then
triple axels! A super-duper falling leaf flip with
extra nuts!

'Ooooh!' The crowd was simply astonished.
'More, more!' they squawked. 'WHAT A
SQUIRREL! WHAT A SHOW! ENCORE!'

This was better than anything ever seen in the
bright lights of Broadway!

Chester whizzed around the fountain one more time. He jumped high, high into the air. The birds put their wings over their eyes. They could not watch. Then Chester landed back upon the ice … and a terrible CRACK! echoed through the park.

Chester's back feet went right through the ice. SPLASH! He was in the freezing water. The birds flapped away in fright, dropping their sunflower seeds as they went.

'Heeelllppp!' called Chester.

'Snowflakes and blizzards!' shouted Pearlie. She whizzed to the icy puddle and offered her wand to help poor Chester out.

Then Pearlie was astonished to find another wand next to hers. She turned to see a fairy dressed warmly in red, white and blue.

It was Crystal the Central Park Fairy!

Between them both, Pearlie and Crystal dragged poor Chester from the freezing depths.

'Phew!' said Chester.

'Yahoo!' yelled Crystal. 'You fell through because the ice is melting, Chester. That means that spring is on its way at last!'

'Way to go!' shouted Misty and Maple as they danced about and gathered the dropped sunflower seeds.

'My stars!' laughed Pearlie.

That night in the squirrels' cosy den, Pearlie and Crystal cooked up a feast of sunflower seed soup, soufflé, donuts and pretzels!

When the squirrels were fast asleep, the two park fairies had a serious talk.

'I can't figure out how the mix-up happened,' said Crystal. 'But as soon as Queen Emerald's ladybird told me I was needed, I flew home as fast as I could.'

'I'm so sorry you had to leave sunny Hawaii,' said Pearlie.

'Are you kidding?' Crystal chuckled. 'I can vacation any time, but there's no finer place to be than Central Park in spring!'

Sure enough, the next morning was fine and sunny and the first shoots of green grass could be seen through the snow.

As the days passed, Crystal and the squirrels showed Pearlie all the wonders of Central Park. She was thrilled to see the buds burst into blossom on every tree.

'Twirly-whirly!' sang Pearlie as she flitted from flower to flower.

'You go, girlfriend!' cheered Crystal.

All too soon it *was* time for Pearlie to go.

Chester, Misty and Maple made an archway
with their furry tails and Pearlie ducked under it.

'We'll miss you like crazy,' said Crystal. She gave
Pearlie a mighty hug.

'And I'll miss you too,' replied Pearlie. 'I'll never
forget Central Park, New York City.'

With a flash of jewelled wings Queen Emerald's ladybird took to the sky with Pearlie aboard. She was looking forward to her next adventure.

Pearlie often visited Central Park in her dreams.
She saw herself curled up in the warm squirrel
den as the snowflakes drifted in silent beauty
around the bare branches of the old oak tree.